Little Agnes & the Ghosts of Kelpie Wharf

STELLA DREXLER

An imprint of Diogenes Club Press

Worldly, Whimsical, and Weird Books

www.diogenesclubpress.com

Dallas, TX

DC Dreams, an imprint of Diogenes Club Press
8619 Reva St. Dallas, TX 74227
www.diogenesclubpress.com

The characters and events in this book are fictional. Any similarity to real persons, living or dead, is coincidental and not intended by the author.

ISBN: 9781622010240
Library of Congress Control Number: 2017955991

Welcome, Honoured Seamen and Esteemed Guests!

To the Port Enshus 305th Annual Aquatic Vertebrae Acquisition Simplification Exposition!

Ingenious Conceptions and Outlandish Innovations Galore!

Featuring the Venerated Dr Nimrod Crowley and the

Revolutionary Mechanical Aquatic Life Demodulator and Seizure Apparatus!

A dense, eerie fog hung over Port Enshus, darkening the mid-morning sky to a dreary, gloomy grey. The air was thick with the chill, salty sea air blowing in from the wharf just south of the village. Everything smelled strongly of fish.

Agnes was tremendously bored. The centre of the the small, stinky seaside village teemed with weathered fishermen and suspiciously well-kept seamen in rich, ill-fitting velvet jackets with long, beaded hair and teeth that glinted gold in the sun. They swaggered around amongst the crowd of crass, noisy village folk like princes among peasants.

Agnes liked pirates. Things always got interesting when pirates showed up to a party, but these pirates were staggeringly disappointing. It didn't even seem as though they intended to loot or pillage anything. Instead, they seemed keen to admire the vendors' ingenious conceptions and outlandish innovations--or, as Agnes liked to think of it, really, really dull fishing stuff. They didn't even leer at anyone.

"Stupid, useless pirates," she muttered.

"Love pirates," Vic moaned, trundling behind her through the crowd, who parted in horror to allow him to pass.

"Not these pirates. They're the worst pirates ever." She paused and looked back at her tall, shambling companion. "Vic! You're all a mess. You're stuck with fishing hooks and things."

He looked down at his raggedy brown suit and mottled grey flesh. His rotting mouth gaped and leered unhappily. "Bait."

Agnes plucked at the glowing, wriggling little fish hooks. They caught in the cadaver's crumbling flesh and tore the old suit. She scowled. "You're arm's coming off again. Vic, how do you get yourself into such straits? Can't you stand a little further away from the sharp, sticky things?"

"Shiny."

She reached into the holster on her belt for a tool to tighten his clockwork arm. A small ginger-haired boy in dirty rags raced past them. He screeched suddenly to a halt and spun back to Agnes and her companion with a disgusted expression that bordered on intense interest.

"What is that thing?" the boy asked, lifting a finger to point at Vic. "Is he a zombie?"

"No! There's no such thing as zombies," Agnes snapped. "That's stupid kiddy stuff. He's a re-animated clockwork cadaver."

"Victim," Vic told the boy sadly.

"I call him Vic," Agnes added. The little boy poked gingerly at Vic. Agnes slapped his hand away. "He isn't a toy."

"Mad science," Vic agreed.

The raggedy little boy spun on his heel and raced away. Agnes rolled her eyes. Typical. "Don't feel bad, Vic. He's just a dreg."

"Ugly." Vic's mouth turned down in a horrible frown.

"Yeah. I hate ginger hair. Come on. I think I see some weapons!"

"Fishing."

"Yeah, but they have to have some sort of really brilliant things here."

The booths were remarkably tedious, but they weren't crowded. In fact, even the most popular booths suddenly emptied of shoppers as Agnes and Vic approached. Agnes toyed with the small, brightly coloured baits shaped like tiny fish that wriggled and glowed as though infused with radioactive life.

"Ew!" They were slimy to the touch, and she scowled at the vendor, an old, salty sailor with a long, greying beard. "What are these things?"

"Uncannily Lifelike Fish Foolery," the vendor announced proudly, gesturing to his squirming wares. "Sure to fool even the cleverest aquatic life."

"That's dumb."

The salty old sailor drew himself up to his fullest, portliest height. "I say, but you are a boorish little girl. What's your name?"

She lifted her chin proudly, and her caramel-coloured pigtails bobbed indignantly through her leather cap. "I'm Agnes Crowley."

"Oh, I–Oh. Begging your pardon, young mistress." The bearded man's cheeks flushed. "Well, my Uncannily Lifelike Fish Foolery may not be as impressive as your father's Revolutionary Mechanical Fish Finder–"

"Aquatic Life Demodulator and Seizure Apparatus," Agnes corrected imperiously.

"Right. Or your...undead friend there." He nodded towards Vic.

4

"He isn't undead! He's a re-animated clockwork cadaver. There is a difference."

His bushy grey eyebrows shot up into his messy fringe. "There is?"

"It's a very fine distinction."

"We are simple folk here in Port Enshus. Your sophisticated modern sciences have yet to reach our humble shores."

Agnes scoffed. "That is quite obvious. Come on, Vic."

"Very rude," Vic told the sailor, waggling a bony, mottled grey finger in disapproval.

The large, brass cage lined with tiny gauges and copper wires was marginally more impressive, but it was intended to trap clawed shellfish and large aquatic mammals, rather than displeasing humans or giant legendary squid. There were large nets woven of glittering metallic mesh, buoys and anchors with sensing devices and demodulators. Haggard old women who smelled of seawater hawked brass goggles with pince nez and spyglass attachments that could see even across the dark, churning waves. Large, decorative brass compasses spun and whirled wildly. There were metal wands with sharp points that looked promising but were only some sort of underwater fish detectors.

Agnes stuck her nose up at a large, cooling unit for storing fish in a ship's hold. She was disappointed in the full-body suits with huge, bulbous metal helmets with hoses and large, mesh eyes for diving. Even the huge, sparkling glass aquarium filled with colourful, exotic fish did not impress the little girl.

They were boring, boring, boring.

"Vic!" Agnes exclaimed in excitement, shoving aside whiny sailors to seize the large, shining gold harpoon on the table before her.

The vendor was a skinny, scraggly man in a pristine white sailor's uniform. He held up his hands. "That's a very dangerous item, little girl—"

She ignored him and lifted the harpoon like a rifle.

"Be careful how you hold that thing—!"

Vic held up his clockwork arms, but his expression was resigned.

"Don't shoot!"

The harpoon made a very satisfying sound as it skewered the air towards Vic. The sharp, jagged point lodged in his chest. He looked down at it in annoyance. "Untoward," he moaned.

"Whoa, that thing is neat!" Agnes exclaimed, jumped forward to yank the harpoon from Vic's rotting chest cavity.

The vendor wrested the harpoon from her hand. His skinny, ratty face flushed with anger. "Give that back! This is not a toy!"

"It looks like a toy."

"I don't know what kinds of toys you play with at home, but this is no place for a reckless, violent little girl! Why don't you go see what sorts of shell necklaces the women are selling?"

Agnes scowled at him in indignation. "I don't like shell necklaces!"

"Well, just get out of here!" He gave her a tiny little shove.

She glared at him, but a large, opaque white globe resting atop a stand constructed entirely of seashells ensnared her attention. "Ooh. Vic, look at this!" She reached to lift the globe, but the vendor, a surly man with a thick belly and grizzled grey hair glared at her through beady eyes.

"Arr, lassie, don't be touchin' the merchandise. It's not for little girls to be playing with."

Agnes drew herself up to her fullest height, which was still barely eye level with the man's scruffy, hirsute collar. "What is it?"

"It be a Concussion-Inducing Exploding Sphere."

"Concussion-Inducing! Exploding!" Agnes beamed at him. Now this was more like it. "What does it do? Does it explode?"

"Aye, it explodes."

"Does it induce concussions?"

"Aye, it does do that, lassie."

"Brilliant!" She paused and lifted an eyebrow. "Fish concussions?"

"Aye, ye be a clever one, lassie. Drop this little beauty in the water, and the concussion ray will send any fish in the area right up to the surface. You can just scoop them up, pretty as you please, and they'll stay nice and quiet for the journey home."

She frowned. "It doesn't kill them?"

"Arr! No, lassie. That would be murder."

"But you catch and eat fish. That's murder, too."

"No, lass, that's survival, that is. We do what we have to do. Besides, the fish are best when kept alive. Fresher, you know."

"Until you kill them."

"To eat them, lass. There's no sport in it."

She glowered in disappointment at the old vendor. "Fishing is boring!"

6

"Hungry," Vic moaned.

"Shut it, Vic. You know you haven't eaten anything in six years."

Her father's voice boomed suddenly through the square. "Honoured seamen, esteemed guests, dear friends and fellow inventors! I require your attention post haste for a most spectacular demonstration!"

She turned towards the makeshift stage where her father spoke into a megaphone, drawing the attention of the sailors, pirates and vendors around them. Dr Nimrod Crowley was an impressive figure. At least, the gulpy fishing townsfolk seemed to think so. They clapped and cheered like vagabonds at a nobbling contest. The doctor was arrayed in sparkling white, and his thick, dark hair struck out at odd angles. He wore dark lenses over his eyes, which gave the curious impression that the man was blind, though Agnes knew her father could see rather better than the townsfolk suspected or the ladies would have been slightly more inclined to adorn themselves in less vulnerable raiment.

Dr. Crowley lifted hands swathed in thick, bright blue rubber gloves, quieting the crowd. He grinned, and his huge, perfect white teeth glinted in the sunlight. "I present, for your appreciation and admiration, the Revolutionary Mechanical Aquatic Life Demodulator and Seizure Apparatus!"

The crowd cheered as Dr Crowley swept a large, white sheet from the apparatus, which resembled a large, patchwork brass ball on a tall, metal stand. It was attached at the end to a long length of rope. The gulpy townsfolk cheered and applauded, though Agnes was sure they had absolutely no idea what the revolutionary dingus even did. She had seen her father's demonstrations before, and she knew the brass ball would open up, forming a large sort of claw that would scoop up the unsuspecting aquatic life unlucky enough to be detected by the demodulator.

So *boring*.

"Imagine, my prestigious friends, never again having to spend days dragging the ocean with old-fashioned, outdated nets! With my marvellous new invention, you will never have to wonder if you are in lucrative waters again!"

Agnes rolled her eyes. He'd practised this speech dozens of times. It was rubbish.

"Now, you may sail carelessly while this clever device senses your catch and scoops it up for you!"

He sounded like an utter fool. Agnes knew the good, simple folk of Port Enshus would hardly understand words like *demodulator, seizure apparatus, applied scientific theory* or *good hygiene*. Nevertheless, it was quite appalling to

7

witness her father stooping to their common, unwashed, fishy-smelling level.

"Come on, Vic," she ordered sourly. "This exposition is about as interesting as listening to a lecture on the care of common household rodents without the satisfaction of listening to methods of extermination. Let's go see what sorts of trouble we can get into in the rest of the town."

"Plebeians," Vic moaned and shambled after her.

Port Enshus was a small village. Very small. Nearly everyone was packed into the tiny town square with the Fish Foolery, Concussion Sphere and Nimrod Crowley's marvellous invention. Around the square, vendors hawked steaming, fishy-smelling food and trinkets made from shining, multi-coloured seashells. It was a quaint little village, despite the bad smell. The people there seemed quite happy, really. It as though the sun shone brightly upon their smiling faces, but there was no sun here in this gloomy town. There was only the salty fog, the whistling of the sea breeze from the wharf and the cheerful shouts and laughter of the honourable seamen and the unsavoury pirates.

The townsfolk gaped at Vic as he shambled beside her along the dark, drear main thoroughfare. He held his mottled, re-animated head high, and Agnes ignored the townsfolk pointedly so they would understand how impolite they were being. Most people were horrified by Vic, but they had the decency to avert their eyes and keep from belting out their alarm.

Most of the shops along the thoroughfare were closed for the exposition, as their proprietors and shop men gathered around the square, selling their wares to whomever might pay them any attention. Only one of the battered, sea-worn shops was noisy with voices and laughter. Agnes poked her head into the small, crowded tavern. Many men and women gathered together or in small groups, sipping steins of ale and grog.

"Minor," Vic moaned.

Agnes ignored him. She pushed inside the dreary, weather-worn wooden tavern and strode up to the bar where a young man with a very long black beard was serving mugs of mead. He lifted a thick, bushy eyebrow at her. "What'll ye have, lass?"

She slapped a hand down on the bar. "Grog." She didn't really know what it was, but it sounded very salty and piratey.

He eyed her suspiciously. "How old are you?"

"Twelve," she replied proudly.

"Oh. Right then." He slammed a stein of thick, dark liquid in front of her.

"Bad choice," Vic argued.

8

She ignored him and tipped the liquid into her mouth. She spat it out in disgust. "Ugh!"

The men and women sitting around her at the bar laughed heartily. She did not like being laughed at, but she liked this grog even less. "How about a nice cider, eh, lass?" the publican suggested.

She nodded and sipped the sweet cider gratefully. She wasn't ready for pirate drinks. Vic followed her into the crowd gathered in the tavern. They weren't seamen, pirates or sailors. All of those were at the expo. Agnes wondered how many of these people actually did an honest day's work. To their credit, they only seemed reasonably horrified by Vic. Anyone with any sense would be, but there was no reason to behave as though her companion was some sort of monster. He was rather politer than most people, living or dead.

"Who's your friend, little one?" a rapscallion in a ratty suit asked as she passed a table of similarly ratty rapscallions.

"This is Vic," Agnes replied cheerfully.

"Never seen anything like him. Is he dangerous?" a woman with long, chestnut brown hair whose terribly crooked, yellowing teeth marred her great beauty.

"I made him in my basement," she explained. "He's not dangerous."

The rapscallions looked at each other in slight alarm. "He looks pretty dangerous."

"Meek," Vic moaned insistently.

"Hear that? He's just a re-animated clockwork cadaver. He can't even bite properly."

"Last time I saw something like him was on Kelpie Wharf," an old, wizened man in a very dark suit announced in a low, wheezing sort of voice.

"Oh, Luther, none of that," the publican complained. "You didn't see anything on Kelpie Wharf."

"I did."

"You didn't."

"I did!"

"You didn't!"

"I did. I did! I DID! And it was right horrible, I tell you!"

Now this was interesting. "What's Kelpie Wharf?" Agnes asked.

Luther grinned through blackened, rotting teeth. "Well, the lassie wants to know about the Wharf. Come, child, sit down beside me, and I'll tell you a tale that'll spook you good and proper."

"I love scary stories!" Agnes kicked out the chair beside Luther and plopped down keenly. Vic lowered himself into the other chair, his clockwork limbs whirring and ticking with each movement.

The rapscallions rolled their eyes, but they leaned forward to listen to Luther's tale. They'd heard it before, but the grog was strong, and Luther's tales were always worth listening to.

"Well, dearie, you are in for a treat." Luther's beady dark eyes glittered. "One night, when I was just a young man, as I was walking along the wharf, I saw something so terrifying, I have never forgotten, not for a moment of my life, even as I forgot my wife's and children's names."

Agnes scoffed. "You forgot your wife and children's names?"

"I must have done. I don't remember them."

"Luther, you old lusher. You ain't never had a wife and children!" the publican growled.

"I did, too!"

"You did not!"

"I did, too! I just forgot them, like I said." He nodded earnestly at Agnes.

"What did you see on the wharf?" she prodded.

"Ah, yes, that. Well, I was just a young man, as I said, a sailor. Back in those days, I was a right brilliant fisherman. Any ship I sailed upon would come home with a full hold and enough food to feed the village for weeks. I tell you, I was brilliant."

She rolled her eyes. "Yeah, yeah. Get on with it."

"Braggart," Vic moaned.

Luther lifted his chin indignantly. "Well, it's true, you know. Anyway, one night I was walking along the wharf. My ship had gone out without me days before, you see, for I had fallen ill."

"A terrible fever he had, mind," one of the rapscallions added. "Delirium."

"I wasn't delirious! I was right proper in my senses, Daniel. You pipe down." Luther turned back to Agnes. "Right, then, I was walking along the wharf when I heard a sort of eerie song."

"A song? Thought you said you heard a whistle," the yellow-toothed woman interjected.

10

"I do not require your helpful commentary, Elaine," Luther snapped. "It was a song. A sort of melody lilting on the salty sea air."

Agnes was not impressed. "Was it a Siren?"

"A what—a what? A Siren? What is that?"

"Don't you dregs ever read books? I bet the pirates know about Sirens, and they can't hardly even spell their own names."

Luther and the rapscallions looked indignant at this, but they were too embarrassed to argue. They didn't read a lot of books in Port Enshus. "It wasn't a Siren. It was a woman."

"Sirens are women. They rise up from the ocean and lure men in with their songs and their beauty and then they devour their souls like bangers. I love bangers." She eyed Luther suspiciously. "Did they devour your soul?"

"No! No, it wasn't a Siren! It was a woman. She was standing at the end of the wharf, near the lighthouse. She glowed and floated like a spectre in the night, but there were no lights anywhere. She was just lit up." His eyes slid away wistfully. "She was the most beautiful woman I ever saw."

Agnes lifted an eyebrow. "I thought you said it was horrible."

"It was horrible, young lady! I am getting there."

"Not very expediently."

"You have to build it up. It's no fun just jumping into it." Luther huffed. "Right, then. There she was, that beautiful, spectral woman, and I thought I was looking straight into my heart's deepest desire."

Agnes interrupted with a scoff. "Your heart's deepest desire is a creepy glowing woman floating on a pier?"

"Maybe it is! There's no shame in that! Anyway, as she floated there, glowing in the dark, foggy night, I moved towards her, my heart thundering as though it might simply leap from my chest."

"Histrionics," Vic moaned.

"A fine thing for you to say, cadaver," Luther snapped. "What do you know about dramatic flair?"

"He knows a lot about that," Agnes said positively. "When he was alive, I think he was some sort of famous thespian. We got him out of a rubbish bin behind a theatre in London."

"Shakespeare," Vic added.

Luther rolled his eyes impatiently. "As I was saying, I moved towards the ghostly woman, and she lifted a hand to beckon me."

11

"What did she look like, Luther?" the publican asked wearily.

"Why, like a vision from my wildest, most intimate dreams. Mind, she was the colour of the moon, but her hair was long and curling, and her face was the sort that could turn a man to drink or suicide with the merest flash of her eyes."

"I thought you said she was ginger before," Elaine put in.

"Shut it, Elaine. She had the fiery passion of a ginger, but I couldn't rightly tell what colour her hair was, could I? She was all pearly and shimmering." He leaned towards Agnes, and his voice dropped. "As I approached her, she never moved, but her song grew louder until I couldn't rightly hear the waves or the ships bobbing in their slips. She filled my eyes and my ears and my senses. Then, when I got close enough to touch her, I reached out a hand to her. That's when--"

"Is this the part where things get horrible?"

"Young lady, you make it very difficult to tell a proper yarn! Yes! That's when things got horrible. Her eyes turned to slits, and her mouth opened on long, sharp, jagged teeth until I was sure she would snap my head right off its stump."

"Your head doesn't sit on a stump. It only becomes a stump when your head's off, right, Vic? Vic knows all about that. See those stitches? We've reattached his head to its stump loads of times. Before that, it was just a neck."

"My neck then! It doesn't much matter! I was certain she was going to bite my head clean off!"

"But she didn't because you still have a head and neck and no stump."

"That is beside the point! I couldn't move. It was like she had trapped me in some sort of force field."

"What, like magnets?"

"No, not like magnets. Like ghosts. A ghost force field."

Agnes considered this. "I suppose a ghost could have a force field, but it would have to be made of matter, not spectre. I suppose ghosts could be made of some sort of plasma or something. Even gases are made of matter. Maybe she was a gas, but gasses don't have significant force fields, really--"

Luther shouted over her. "As I was saying! I couldn't move, and then her song turned into a scream, and I could feel the sound reverberating inside my body as though it would be blasted apart by the noise. Dreadful, it was. It was as though she was singing my death."

"Banshee," Vic put in helpfully.

"Yeah. Yeah, Luther, it does sound a lot like a banshee," one of the rapscallions remarked.

Luther thought about this. "Yeah. Yeah, I suppose she might have been a banshee."

"But banshees foretell your death. You aren't dead."

"Not yet, I'm not! But when I see the banshee woman again, I know she will be the last thing I ever see in this world."

"What makes you think you will see her again?" Agnes asked.

"She's the Ghost of Kelpie Wharf."

"She ain't, either," the publican argued. "No one else has ever seen her."

"But they've seen other things. She might come to everyone in different forms. Maybe the form that attracts them or scares them the worst."

They all thought about this. "How did you get away, though?" Agnes demanded. "I thought you said she was singing your death."

"She was. I could feel it. It was coming. My head felt bursting to explode. But then, just as I thought I couldn't bear it anymore, I heard a foghorn in the distance. My ship had come home. The lighthouse illuminated, and it flashed across the wharf. The banshee woman gave a last shriek, which felled me to my knees, and then she leapt over the railing and disappeared into the water."

Everyone was silent a moment. Agnes peered contemplatively into her cider. "But no one else has ever seen her? Maybe you imagined it."

"I didn't imagine it! There are ghosts; anyone will tell you. And I saw one! And she was horrible, and she was going to kill me. It was only my crew coming to port that saved my life that night."

"Luther, that never happened. There's no Ghost of Kelpie Wharf," the publican growled.

Suddenly, another voice rose in the din of the argument. It was soft, but it carried over the crowd with uncanny clarity. "There is," the young woman said. "I saw it. But it wasn't a woman. It wasn't anything like that."

Agnes swivelled in her seat to peer at the young woman. She was shockingly thin and pale, as fragile as porcelain. She looked eerily haunted, terribly sad, and Agnes could surely believe there were ghosts lurking around this woman. "What did you see?" she breathed keenly.

"Sarah, don't," Elaine said in a voice that was curiously kind.

Sarah waved her hand. "It's all right. I saw the ghost, but it wasn't a woman, and it wasn't the middle of the night. It was a dark day, foggy like today." She took a hitching breath, and her gaunt shoulders trembled. Her voice was a pale, reedy whisper. "Just like today."

"What did it look like?" Agnes pressed.

"It was not a woman. It was a man."

"Sarah…" Elaine murmured.

"Did you know him?"

Sarah shook her head. "No, I didn't know him. But it was…it was like Luther said, though I couldn't see his face at all. He just…stood there, on the wharf. He was alone. He was looking out over the sea, as though he was looking for something. There was something about him…I knew he wasn't a normal man. He sort of shimmered and shifted like the fog, and I could almost see the sea straight through him.

"Suddenly I felt as though if I did not go straight to him, I would simply die. He drew me, so forcibly I thought my heart would surely burst if I did not get close to him. It was as though he embodied everything I had ever wanted or dreamed. And so I moved closer, and then…" She took a hitching breath and suddenly seized her head as though it was paining her greatly.

Elaine reached over and squeezed Sarah's frail shoulder. "It's all right, Sarah."

"No, it isn't!" Agnes snapped. "I want to hear the rest of the story."

"Climax," Vic added mournfully.

Sarah looked up through her thin fingers. She sighed. "All right. I got closer, and I reached for him, and then…then he spun suddenly upon me, and I saw he wasn't a man at all but a beast with horrible, white flesh, long, sharp teeth and huge, wild eyes. He came at me, and I stumbled back, but it was too late. He leapt upon me, and I…"

Agnes slapped the table with her hand as Sarah choked off again. Sarah jumped in alarm. "What happened? Finish the story."

"That is the end. I fainted dead away, and when I woke up, he was gone, but…"

"Did he do something to you?"

"No, not that I know of. I must have hit my head, but I was all right. Nothing had happened to me. I don't know…I don't know if he went away when I fainted or if someone came to rescue me. No one ever claimed to know anything about it, but…something must have stopped him."

They all considered this in silence a moment, but no one scorned Sarah or insisted her story was a lie. She looked as though she might shatter to pieces or shards of white glass at the merest harsh word or strong breath.

"What's on that wharf," a man with a thick black beard and startling blue eyes added darkly from a corner, "is a not a ghost. It's a monster."

They all turned to him in surprise. "Matty? What do you know about it?" the publican demanded. He was quite alarmed, for Matty rarely spoke to anyone, not since the night his wife had cast herself out to sea.

"I know my wife didn't throw herself off that pier that night. Something took her." Matty's eyes were shadowed by the wide-brimmed black hat upon his head, but he swept it off his head and stared around at the shocked patrons with glittering intensity.

Agnes was quite delighted by this unexpected turn. These people were far more interesting and far gulpier than she'd imagined. "What happened to her?"

"Denial," Vic moaned.

She nudged him. "Do shut up, Vic. Let the man tell his story."

"Matty?" Luther asked, lifting bushy, grizzled eyebrows.

Matty inclined his head. He was not an old man, but there were deep lines around his eyes, as though he'd aged quickly and harshly. "Evangeline was...a troubled woman, but she would not have taken her life. No one would have believed me, not the constable or the town council, but I followed her to the pier that night."

"You were there, Matty?" Sarah asked softly. "But you never said."

"No, well, of course not. How do you think that would have looked? Everyone knew Evangeline and I rowed constantly. They would have blamed me for her death. It was not I who killed her. It was the Ghost. It dragged her down into the water, and she never came back up. Not until morning, and by then...by then she was dead."

Agnes' eyes widened in glee. "Did the ghost kill her?"

Matty inclined his head. "She woke in the middle of the night, and I heard her leave the house. I feared she might have fallen into one of her fits, and so I followed her to the wharf. It was dark and still and clear that night, so I was not mistaken in what I saw. She walked along the pier, looking out at the sea, and I thought she would be all right. Perhaps she needed air, for we'd rowed that night, and I think she wanted to be alone. I did not approach her or call to her that I was there." He squeezed his eyes shut, passing a large, burly hand over his eyes.

"What did you see, Matty?" Luther asked.

"It was so sudden, there was nothing I could do. One moment she was there, standing alone on the wharf, her long hair blowing out behind her, and the next—and the next something shimmering and serpentine rose out of the water. She did not even scream. She looked at the thing, and then it reached for her, wrapping its long, scaly arms around her, and dragged her down into the water. I ran to her, to catch her or bring her back, but there was nary a ripple on the surface of the water. There was no sign of her or of the creature that had stolen her from me."

There was a breathless pause. "What did you do, Matty?" Elaine whispered.

"I went in after her. I climbed down the rigging, and I dove into the water, but though I called her name over and over, and I dove down as deeply as I could without losing myself, I could not find her. She'd simply vanished. I waited there for hours, until the first grey light of dawn rose on the horizon. And then...and I then I went home. It was afternoon when the constable came to tell me they'd discovered her body. There was no sign of the monster's presence at all. They suspected she'd simply leapt from the wharf and was dashed on the rocks below. No one ever claimed to have seen the creature again."

"Dreadful," Vic told Matty sympathetically.

"Yes," Matty breathed, leaning back over his stein, and nothing more could be coaxed from the man. He slipped back into his solitary silence, leaving an awkward, desolate mood in his wake.

"I saw something else," a young woman said meekly, and everyone spun to look at her.

"Another ghost?" Agnes asked keenly. This was loads of fun.

"Yes, but it wasn't a monster and it wasn't a grey lady. It was Rufus."

"Rufus?" asked the publican with sharp scepticism.

"Yes, Rufus!" snapped the woman. She looked the sensible sort, dressed in a very plain, no-nonsense dress of drab brown. Her long, auburn hair was twisted into a severe bun. She was not, by any appearance, mad, though her subsequent words belied this impression.

"Rufus?" Vic repeated.

"My dog," she explained imperiously, lifting her chin at the looks of incredulous disdain on the faces of her fellow patrons. "He died several years ago, you see, and I was quite heart-broken at his loss. He was my closest and dearest companion, a wolf dog whom I had raised from a pup. Never were we apart, and he was allowed even to accompany me to the homes in which I was employed as governess."

16

"You saw the ghost of your dog?" Agnes was not impressed by this story, for dogs were very boring, even ghostly dogs.

"Yes, I did! I was taking a walk on the wharf one afternoon, hoping to catch a glimpse of the ships coming to port, but there were no sails on the horizon, so I paused a moment to enjoy the fresh air. That is when I saw him. He came out of nowhere, but I knew it was him, for I would have known his scent and his presence had I been blind. He ran across the pier, and I called to him, but he did not answer me as he had when he was alive. He merely kept running, and so I followed him. He reached the edge of town, just on the border of the pier, but he seemed unable to go any further.

"I called to him and approached, hoping at least to tell him how I had missed him so, but he turned upon me, and his eyes were not the warm, sweet brown they had once been. Instead, they glowed a terrible red, and he drew back his teeth to give me the most ferocious and terrifying snarl. I was shocked, for he had never treated me so, and though I knew for certain it was him, I realized that death had changed him.

"I stepped away, but he stalked towards me and then he stopped and threw his head back, letting out the most fearsome howl I have ever heard. I knew that my life was in danger from the creature I had once cherished above all others and who had adored me unconditionally. I turned and I ran, and I could hear his panting and smell his horrible, sulphurous breath like brimstone." She took a hitching breath, and her eyes slid away as she relived the terrible memory. "But then, just as I felt him bearing down on me, he was gone. Just like that. As suddenly as he had appeared."

"Did you ever see him again?" Luther asked, for he had never seen his beautiful banshee woman, nor had Sarah or Matty seen their monsters.

"No. I never did. I avoid Kelpie Wharf now, if I can. But even when I have been along the pier, awaiting the sailors, I have never seen sign of my beloved companion again."

A beautiful, terrible woman, a fanged man, a murderous sea monster, a feral dog—were they all ghosts, or was there only one who could change its shape at will? Agnes thought about this for a long moment. These people could, perhaps, all be round the bend. There could be a collective madness that had swept through the town with the fog, but that was no reason not to believe them, for ghosts were quite exciting, even if they were only composed of shape-shifting gasses.

"Same ghost?" Vic seemed to be thinking the same thing.

Everyone in the tavern considered this. "It could be," Luther admitted.

"Perhaps it takes the shape of what you...what you want or fear most. Perhaps it can take your desires and twist them into evil creatures."

"But there is no such thing as ghosts," one of the rapscallions insisted disdainfully. "It's all phooey and rubbish and creativity."

"It isn't, either!" Matty snapped. "I saw that thing, and it took my Evangeline. You can't tell me that is phooey and rubbish. I saw it!"

The rapscallion lifted an eyebrow. "Did you really? Or was it perhaps that you had had a bit too much of the wormwood that night and your mind turned your wife's suicide into something more...palatable?"

"Now, Thomas, that is no sort of thing to say," Luther scolded. "If Matty says saw the creature, he saw the creature."

"That doesn't mean it's not a figment of his imagination."

"And my banshee? That was figment?"

"You're barmy, old man. I wouldn't be the least surprised that you're seeing things."

"Young man, you would do well to speak more respectfully to your elders," snapped Luther.

Thomas rolled his eyes. "Right. Well, in any case, I don't believe in ghosts. Everyone has a story about Kelpie Wharf, but no one has ever seen the same creature. It's all what they want to see, perfectly tailored ghosts that fulfil their deepest desires. You saw the woman of your dreams, Lily saw her lost dog. Matty imagined a death for his wife that carried no shame. It's hysteria, I tell you. Collective mass hysteria. It's in all the head books."

"Since when have you been reading head books?" Elaine demanded, appalled.

"There's loads you lot don't know about me," Thomas replied proudly. "I read a lot of books."

"Well, that's just pseudoscience and theory," Agnes scoffed. "That doesn't prove anything. There could be ghosts."

"Little girl, don't let these mad lushers fill your head with foolish nonsense," Thomas said austerely. "It will do you little good. You'd be better served picking up a book."

Agnes rolled her eyes. "I'm a genius, I'll have you know, sir. Why, I brought a cadaver to life with a Van der Graff generator, several straight pins and a few clockworks when I was six. I think I know the difference between gulpy hysterics and sensible scientific reasoning." She rose from her seat, though her diminutive stature somewhat failed to impress upon her audience the intended imperiousness of the gesture. "And I intend to conduct an experiment and form my own conclusions. Come along, Vic. We're going ghost hunting."

"Foggy," Vic complained, though he shambled to his feet beside her.

"Don't fret. The moisture won't improve your smell, but you're looking a bit husky. You'll be all right. Just don't fall in the water; you'll rust your gears."

"Little girl, Kelpie Wharf is no place for children," Luther scolded. "You should not be doing any such thing."

"I am Agnes Crowley, and I go where I please." She pushed aside her long, brown leather jacket to reveal the bulbous glass pistol on her hip. "Besides, I have a death ray. Even a gassy ghost can't escape the awesome power of directed energy particles intent on vaporising their ethereal bits."

"Well, this I've got to see," Luther remarked and pushed laboriously to his feet. He grinned toothlessly around at the tavern patrons. "To Kelpie Wharf!"

* * *

Kelpie Wharf was dismal and grey. The fog, so dense and moist with the salty sea air, was oppressive and choking. A spooky stillness hung over the silent ships bobbing in their slips. Agnes listened in the thick, eerie silence, but there was no snarling, splashing or singing from the legendary ghost.

She crept stealthily along the creepy, soggy, battered wooden pier, but the locals trailing behind her, whispering urgently to each other, destroyed any hope of taking the ghosts unawares. She could see nothing through the grey murk, no glimmer or faint glow in the darkness. If there was a ghost of Kelpie Wharf, it seemed disinclined to brave the desolate haze.

When it came, what would it be for her? Would it be shambling clockwork cadavers like Vic? Angry, helpless minions like Hector? Or would it be Ambrose, her one true love...No, it wouldn't be Ambrose. He wasn't dead, after all, and he wasn't here to be snatched away by a sea monster. She didn't have any dead pets—well, unless she counted laboratory rats and the other disastrous experimental animal-like creations she and her father had cooked up in their laboratory. She shivered deliciously, enjoying the frisson of fear that chased down her spine at the thought.

It wasn't anything. She didn't see anything. Even the sea was quiet below, and the empty ships merely looked sad, not spooky. She huffed indignantly and spun to face the barmy shanty-townspeople who had trailed her from the tavern. She scowled at them.

"This is just a wind-up, isn't it?" she demanded. "It's a sham. You were all just making up stories to frighten me."

"Oh, no," Luther murmured softly, peering around with a sort of reverent terror in his watery eyes. "It's true. It's all true. Perhaps we...perhaps only one person can see it at a time. Perhaps the ghost doesn't know what to become because there are too many of us here."

Agnes scowled. "That's rubbish. This whole thing is rubbish. There's no ghost of Kelpie Wharf!"

But it wasn't rubbish, for, as she spoke, something shimmered in the murk ahead. "There!" she cried abruptly. Without thinking, as was customary, Agnes spun and raced after the creature. It was large and, though it was oddly shiny, it was deep, Stygian black, something with long limbs and sharp claws, something that moved as though it was slithering in through the fog.

"Why is it running away?" Agnes demanded as the creature bounded away from her through the fog, leaping onto the roofs of the weathered, trembling shanties lining the wharf before disappearing into the grey.

Agnes stopped abruptly at the edge of the pier, staring frantically out over the water. She'd not heard a splash, but the long, glimmering black creature had simply vanished over the side of the wharf, into the murk below. "It's gone! Where did it go?" She marched back to the locals, scowling.

"You saw it?" Luther asked breathlessly.

"Didn't you?"

"No. I just saw you run into the fog. That was very foolish, lass. It could have dragged you down into the sea like poor Evangeline."

"It wouldn't have done any such thing," Agnes scolded him. "Ghosts can't do that if they're just made of gasses and ether. Anyway, it didn't look like gas or a ghost. It was black. Pure black."

"Is that so? Odd, that. Did you know the thing?"

"Of course I didn't know it! It was a weird shiny black ghost thing!"

"Well, you do run about with a re-animated clockwork cadaver, lass. Stranger things have been observed."

She rolled her eyes. "Why did it run away? Do ghosts run away? They're dead. They have nothing of which to be afraid."

Luther lifted his shoulders, but it was Elaine who spoke. "You did mention the awesome power of your weaponry. It might have heard you."

Agnes scoffed. "It wasn't even around then. That was a private conversation."

"Perhaps ghosts listen on different wavelengths than humans," Luther suggested feebly.

Agnes leaned over the railing, staring down at the still, quiet sea below. She huffed. There was no sign of the creature, though she was certain it had gone over the rail. Could it have been a ghost or was it simply another twisted, barmy denizen of this strange, creepy grey shanty-town? She spun. "Vic? What do you reckon?"

Vic's gears whirred as he lifted his clockwork shoulders. "Jack?"

"What? What the hell does that mean?"

"Spring."

Agnes frowned at him. "Are your bits running down again? Do you need oiled?"

His bulging, lifeless eyes rolled in his head. "Kelpie."

"Vic, stop talking rubbish."

Her attention was drawn, however, by a sudden cacophony of noise that pierced the murky stillness of the wharf. They spun to find the townspeople racing from town towards the wharf. She blinked in surprise and hurried to Luther's side as he threw himself against the railing beside her.

"What on earth is going on?" she demanded.

Luther lifted a hand to point out to sea. "The ships! The men are home!"

She hadn't noticed the two tall ships moving slowly towards the wharf. She frowned. "Hasn't anyone turned on the light for them?"

"No. We didn't hear their foghorns. Strange, that, but I suppose in all the excitement of the expo and that apparition you saw..."

Agnes frowned, peering out at the ships. "But, that's quite peculiar."

Luther ignored her. He turned his head to call out to the rapscallions who'd followed them. "Boys! Tell the crier the Aqueous Spectre and the Wraith Alloy have come home!"

The town crier was swift and noisy. Agnes could hear him racing through the streets, into the square with his joyful shouts of, "They're home! Our men are home! The ships are coming to port!"

The crowd pressed against Agnes, Vic and Luther as the townspeople rushed to the wharf to meet their men. Their exuberance was excessive. The ships glided slowly and serenely to port, but there was something odd about them. Agnes knew very little about nautical ships, for her father insisted on travelling by air, but they moved towards the wharf almost aimlessly, as though their captains were napping behind the steering mechanisms. They did not collide, but once, their noses bumped ever gently against each other, sending them both careening

21

slowly away.

The cheers and whooping of the crowd died down, and they waited in breathless anticipation for their men to return to them. Agnes, too, was curious despite her complete apathy towards the denizens of Port Enshus.

The ships moved nearer the port, and the whispering began. Something was wrong.

"What's going on?" Agnes asked Luther.

The grizzled old man frowned out at the sea. "I don't know. They aren't moving like they're 'sposed to."

"I could have told you that. It's obvious, and I know as much about ships as I do about gassy ghosts."

"Where are they?" The murmur spread through the crowd into a crescendo of nervous shouts.

"What is it?" Agnes demanded.

"The men. They aren't there on the deck."

Agnes squinted through the dense murk and spotted what the others had seen—or rather, failed to see. No sailors stood upon the deck, leaning over the railing to wave cheerfully at the townspeople who awaited them so expectantly.

She waited, breathless, with the people of Port Enshus as the two ships moved ever closer, so slowly it seemed as though they might stop, bobbing aimlessly, before they ever made it to port. Eventually, the smaller of the two ships, its side emblazoned with Wraith Alloy in gold script, slid into port, but it did not slide gracefully into its slip. Instead, it bumped softly against the railing of the wharf and simply stopped.

"But there's no one there." The whispers began again, and the Aqueous Spectre collided with the Wraith, shaking the wharf at their feet.

"What's happened?"

"Are they below?"

"Why hasn't anyone come out?"

"Who is steering the ship?"

"No one's steering it. They've all gone!"

"What's going on?"

The crowd surged forward. "Hello? Is anyone there?"

A young, sturdy-looking boy with bright, blue eyes and shaggy blonde hair stepped forward. "I'll go below and see what's keeping them."

"Wait—" Agnes called, but her voice was drowned by the noisy crowd.

"Rash," Vic added beside her, looking quite grim despite his perpetual leer.

The hasty shanty-townspeople were paying them no heed. The young boy and his eager companions dropped ropes down the side of the wharf and hoisted themselves over the railing.

There was nothing else for it. Agnes fumbled at the tool belt on her waist and found the tiny, retractable brass megaphone she kept for just such occasions. "Everybody hold your horses!"

Her voice boomed over the crowd, and they fell suddenly quiet, murmuring to themselves. The boys stopped dead in their tracks, looking around for the source of the voice. When they spotted Agnes yanking a gas mask over her small, heart-shaped face, they gaped at her in surprise.

"I am Agnes Crowley," she declared. "Daughter of Dr Nimrod Crowley, and I order you to stop what you are doing! It is not safe to go down on that ship."

"What?"

"Why?"

"We have to find out what happened to our men!"

"Pipe down! There are only a few reasons two ships come to port with no captain and no sailors. One of them is plague."

The word was like the crack of a whip. The boys scrambled back onto the wharf, racing back towards the centre of town as though they might escape the sailor's horrible fate.

"Plague?"

"Certainly not!"

"But that's been extinct for years!"

"Foolish little girl."

"What if she's right?"

"Send someone down!"

"Where is my husband?"

"Where is my son?"

"Everyone shut up!" Luther snarled. "Little Agnes, what do you suggest we do?"

She beamed at him, but he could not tell, for her mouth was obscured by the gas mask. "Well, we'll send Vic down. He's not alive, just re-animated, so he can't get the plague."

"Figures," Vic moaned.

"Yes!"

"Perfect!"

"Send the zombie!"

"He's not a zombie!" Agnes snapped. She jerked her head at her re-animated clockwork cadaver. "Go on, then, Vic."

"Rats." He curled his lip resentfully, but it was difficult to tell the difference between it and his usual gaping grin, so Agnes did not trouble herself. She watched him eagerly as he lurched over the side of the wharf, struggling gracelessly down the young men's ropes. He lumbered onto the deck of the Wraith and disappeared into the cabin. The crowd waited on tenterhooks for him to emerge, holding scarves or shawls over their noses and mouths as though it might prevent the spread of the terrible plague, should their men have carried it across the sea with them.

Finally, after several long, breathless moments, Vic's rotting, grinning face appeared from the ship's cabin. His expression gave nothing away, but Agnes seemed satisfied. She nodded as he shambled back up onto the deck.

"Well?"

"What did you see?"

"Are they down there?"

"Are they dead?"

"Are they sleeping?"

"Gone," Vic moaned, gripping the rope to climb back up to the wharf.

"Gone? What do you mean 'gone?'"

"Vanished."

"They can't have vanished! Where could they have gone?"

"Maybe it is a new plague! A plague that makes people vanish!"

"No!"

"The horror!"

"Everyone run away!"

Agnes rolled her eyes. "Everyone shut your faces! There's no such thing as a plague that makes you vanish. I will go down to the ship and see what is going on." She hoisted herself over the railing and climbed down to meet Vic, who reached up, whirring and ticking, to help her down onto the slightly swaying wooden deck. "Those bunch of gulpy scaredy-cats."

Vic nodded in agreement. "Parochial."

"They're really not here?"

He shook his head, following her grudgingly back down into the cabin. She frowned around. There was no sign of the sailors or the ship's captain, but the cabin looked pleasantly homey. There were bunks lining the walls, covered with the sailor's meagre personal items: pictures tacked to the walls above their pillows, blankets piled high, books and writing utensils, decks of cards and pick-up sticks. There were small, inane mementos and knick-knacks, which Agnes took as signs of sentimental sailors, whom, she was certain, would not have left them behind, unless they had been forced to hastily abandon ship.

The remnants of dinner still remained in the mess hall, and Agnes frowned around at the cramped, rounded wooden room. The empty long tables and benches looked eerily wrong somehow. A pot of stew still steamed in the tiny galley. "They were in the middle of dinner. There's no plague here. This is something else."

"Bermuda."

"Rubbish. We're nowhere near the Caribbean. Something else happened here, and I intend to find out what it was. Are you with me, Vic?"

"Shackled."

"So we're all in. Come on, let's see if the same thing happened to the other ship. We're going to find out what happened to these sailors."

"Did you find them?"

"Are they there?"

"Are they all dead?"

"What's happening?"

"Little girl, tell us what you found!"

Agnes held up her hand to the crowd. "I'm sorry, but everyone is gone."

"Gone?"

"I already said that! Don't start. There is no plague here, but something has caused your men to simply disappear."

"The ghosts!"

"The ghosts of Kelpie Wharf have taken them!"

"Argh! Not the ghosts!"

"There's no such thing as ghosts!"

Agnes frowned at them. "Everyone pipe down. This is no time for hysterics."

She wondered if the sailors' disappearance could be connected to the figure she saw bounding across the wharf. It didn't seem likely. The figure had been on the wharf, after all, while the ships were still out to sea. She did not credit the idea that a single figure, regardless of its matter construct or purported meta-physicality could cause some fifty or a hundred men to simply vanish into the open sea with no sign at at all, especially when that figure was nowhere near the scene of the crime.

It might have been pirates or slavers, she supposed, but how had they managed to snatch up so many men without even a tiny fight, for the mess hall and the cabins looked as though no struggle had ever occurred within their walls, was beyond her reasoning. Besides, most of the pirates were in the town square, admiring her father.

"What will we do?"

"We must find them!"

"Where is my husband?"

"Rory Everett said he was going to marry me! Is this some sort of way to welch on our deal?"

"Everyone calm down!" Agnes scowled imperiously at them, her fists propped on her hips. "You are being ridiculous. We're going to search the other ship and see if we can uncover any clues. You lot just stay here and keep it down. You're giving me a migraine."

"Silly," Vic added, waggling a scolding finger at them as the they climbed up the rigging to the Aqueous Spectre, which, having simply crashed unceremoniously into the Wraith Alloy, was quite easily accessible. There was little to be found. It looked much the same, though the dinner still steaming on the crew's plates was bangers and mash. Agnes gazed thoughtfully at the uncannily empty benches.

"Captain," Vic moaned.

She nodded slowly. "Yes, let's check the captain's quarters. There might be something interesting there. Maybe he's a mad scientist and slipped some sort of shrinking potion into the crew's dinner."

"Cook?"

"Yes, you're right. The cook would have to be in on it. Perhaps the cook's our man. Or both cooks and captains were conspiring together to create an army of miniature sailors to battle each other so the villains could place bets!"

"Outlandish."

"Stranger things have happened, Vic. Look at you."

26

But when they located the captain's quarters, it was as completely deserted as the mess hall. A plate piled high with the captain's dinner lay upon the ornate, polished wood table set into the wall.

"Well, that's right out," she sighed in disappointment. "Something really weird is going on here. We'd better tell the townspeople their men are gone."

"Sad."

"Oh, they'll get over it in time." She rubbed her chin thoughtfully. "Although, am sure there is nothing that happened here that cannot be explained by simple science. There must be some explanation for this mysterious phenomenon."

"Kelpies."

"No." She stomped her foot. "I do not think the ghosts got them. Although...I did see something very strange on the wharf."

"Scared?"

"I was not scared! Anyway, I am sure there is some perfectly reasonable explanation for all of this."

"Dr Crowley."

"No way. I'm not letting him in on this. He will take all the fun and glory out of it. Besides, he's busy smarming the fishy dregs and revelling in his genius. It's up to us to solve this mystery." She huffed, then she looked at him with raised eyebrows. "Now, how are we going to solve this mystery?"

Vic lifted his shoulders. "Evidence?"

"Gee, that's helpful." She scowled thoughtfully around the cabin. "Although...Ah ha!" She snatched up a battered leather journal resting on the slightly swaying nightstand.

"Diary?"

"Captain's log." Agnes frowned over the neat, spidery scrawl. "The last entry was about an hour ago. They were about a kilometre from land, preparing to come to port. Whatever happened to them, it happened not long ago." She slapped the captain's log against Vic's chest. "Hold this. Let's check the other ship."

They ignored the shouts and supplications from the Port Enshions on the wharf and climbed down the rigging to the Aqueous Spectre. Its master had not been as neat or meticulous as the captain of the Wraith Alloy, but he had notated their proximity to the Spectre at nearly the same moment.

"Vic, something untoward happened to these ships, and we are going to discover what it is."

"Sit out."

"Stop complaining. Anything is better than mucking about in this fishy shanty town. Step lively."

He shambled after her as she climbed back up to the wharf, facing the anxious townspeople with her hands on her hips.

"People of Port Enshus, I know what has happened to your men!"

"What?"

"Was it plague?"

"Kelpies!"

"Pirates!"

"Slavers!"

"Shipwreck!"

"The ships aren't wrecked!"

"They were thrown overboard!"

"Who could have thrown them overboard?"

"Pipe down, you lot!"

"What was it, little girl? What happened to the sailors?"

"Well, I don't...I don't know for sure."

"You said you knew!"

"Lies!"

"We trusted you!"

Agnes raised her voice to be heard over the crowd before they dissolved into another foolish tirade. "All right, all right, I might have exaggerated. I do not know what happened to them. But I knew when and where it happened!"

"Where did it happen?"

"When did it happen?"

"Was it the ghosts?"

"Did the slavers get them?"

"Will my husband be forced to scrub toilets?"

"Well, I don't know exactly where and when, but I know nearly where and when." She drew herself up to her fullest height. "Dregs of Port Enshus, I require the fastest boat in the village. Or, preferably, your most sophisticated aerostat."

The people of Port Enshus glanced at each other in confusion. "Aerostat?"

She rolled her eyes. "A boat will do. Step lively, you lot! I will solve the mystery of your missing men!"

"Huzzah!"

"Hooray!"

"Three cheers for the little girl!"

"Are you quite sure this is wise?"

"But you're only a little girl."

Agnes glared around at the crowd. "Only a little girl? I'll have you know, I am Agnes Crowley, prodigious progeny of the infamous and venerable Dr Nimrod Crowley. I have battled the wild East End Troubadour Troop; braved the Clockwork Cornucopia; and bested the Malodorous Savage Eutherian Vic smuggled into his casket. I solved the mysteries of the Wailing Phantasmal Debutante and the Ubiquitous Radioactive Elaterid. I am confident I am quite suited to the challenge. Now, dregs! Bring me a boat!"

"Bring this little girl a ship!"

They scattered, chattering like monkeys. Agnes beamed smugly around at them as they scrambled to purvey her vessel.

"Little Agnes! Little Agnes!" The rapscallions motioned her from a small, gleaming wooden jolly boat floating quietly in the water below. She hooted gleefully and leapt over the railing. Water lapped against the glass hull, and small fish peered curiously up at Vic as he lumbered down onto the polished deck. "Welcome aboard the Brass Canary," Thomas told them proudly. "The fastest ship in Port Enshus!"

Agnes seized the large, gleaming brass hand-wheel. She didn't know very much about boats, but she checked the domed gauges on the helm as though she could read them perfectly. She lifted her chin. "It is quite acceptable. I shall return with the men post haste. Now, please get off my ship."

Thomas opened his mouth to protest. Vic lifted a hand to shove the loquacious rapscallion into the tranquil waves. He spluttered, but Agnes added some coal to the boiler, and the Brass Canary sliced swiftly across the bay. She whooped in delight.

"This boat is fast!"

"Compass."

"I know how to read a compass!"

"Foolish."

"You shut your face. I know what I'm doing. We'll find these sailors in no time."

"Dubious."

"Your attitude is becoming increasingly unsupportive. Do you require an adjustment?"

Vic blanched. "Spot on."

She smirked. "That is much better."

They did not encounter any ships as they sped over the serene waters. Agnes checked the gauges, hoping they were steering her in the direction in which the Wraith Alloy and Aqueous Spectre had fallen victim to the mysterious circumstances. She glanced out over the water.

"Land."

Agnes blinked in surprise, looking around. Vic was right. A small copse of trees appeared so suddenly on the horizon, she thought perhaps she was imagining them. But, no, the trees were there, forming a wall around the tiny island in the middle of the sparkling blue waters. "Vic! You're right! I think it's an island!"

"Deserted?"

"Mm. I don't know." She checked the gauges in front of her. "But these are the right coordinates. I believe this island might tell us something about what happened to those men."

"Imprudent."

She waved her hand dismissively. "What's a bit of danger? I've got my merry side arm, and I'm keen for some adventure." She spun the wheel dramatically, steering towards the mysterious island.

"Oversized beasts."

"Come now, Vic, that's nothing more than fiction and fancy. There are no genetically engineered monsters here."

The Brass Canary drew gently ashore, and Vic alighted gracelessly on the grey sand. He didn't reach a hand to assist Agnes out of the vessel. He gestured around him. "Pirates?"

She glanced around the quiet, tranquil island. She could hear birds singing in the distance, but there were no boot prints, no scattered bones or broken bottles, no ruckus to indicate a pirate crew or slaver vessel was anywhere nearby. "I think not. I daresay a cursory investigation will uncover this mystery. Let us be off!"

The island's vegetation was lush and verdant, but Agnes and her clockwork companion paid it no heed. The Crowleys and their uncanny creations had never formed an appreciation of the beauties of untrodden wilderness. This island was not prey to the aggressive murk that plagued Port Enshus, but the sky was gloomy grey. A thin mist crept along the forest floor, obscuring the once colourful blossoms that now looked shrivelled and withered under the haze.

Agnes paused in a small, murky clearing, scowling around at the dense fauna. Vic stumbled into her, muttering irritably under his breath. She propped her hands up on her hips. "I don't see any sailors around here, Vic."

He made a curious rumbling sound in response, but when she turned to look sharply at him, he looked as mystified by the noise as she.

"What was that?"

"Quake."

"I know it was a quake! But what caused it?" Her dark amber eyes lit with acuity. "The sailors."

Vic peered at her with a leer that clearly communicated his doubt.

"Whatever caused that tremor, it wasn't nature. There's something here on this island, Vic, and we are going to discover it."

He lifted his shoulders in the undead approximation of a sigh, for his uncanny body no longer drew breath.

Agnes listened closely, but there was no further trembling from the forest floor. She sighed in disappointment, and they edged closer to shore.

Behind her, Vic chattered relentlessly in several different voices that sounded nothing like this own.

Agnes spun to him, scowling. "What was that?"

He lifted his hands in bemusement.

She narrowed her eyes. "That's it." She dropped to the dank floor, mindless of the pretty day red day dress her father had insisted she wear to the exposition. She fumbled at her belt for a small, brass trumpet that she pressed to her ear. The other end of the trumpet narrowed to a long, rubber hose terminating at a large, concave disc, with which she scanned the ground, listening for the ceaseless chatter.

There it was. She could hear dozens of voices, all of them talking rubbish. She followed the sound with her trumpet, Vic trundling behind her, stumbling over the exposed roots and fallen branches. The sound came to a sudden crescendo, and she looked keenly around for an entrance into the underground cocktail party.

She could see none. She walked several more paces, but the noises dampened suddenly. She cursed most unlike a lady of breeding. She returned to the spot she had heard the voices most clearly, but a second inspection yielded no greater insights regarding the entrance.

Suddenly, a high-pitched cackle rent the thick, eerie quiet above ground.

Vic let out a quiet grunt heavy with alarm.

Agnes spun towards the sound in time to see an uncannily tall man with skin as ivory pale as porcelain bounding towards them in unnaturally high leaps. His face, long and pointed like a devil's, was flat and almost featureless, though large eyes burned red out of the slight indentations of his eye sockets. His mouth was a ragged, gaping slash with sharp, pointed teeth. The creature wore naught but a ratty, torn black shirt and trousers.

"What is that?" Agnes demanded, fumbling for her tool belt.

"Terror of London!" Vic squeaked.

She turned a scathing glare upon her companion. "Certainly he isn't either! Don't be ridiculous."

But the creature certainly looked like the sprightly master of menace, the thing of nightmares, tall tales and legends told in the darkest hours of night. It leapt several metres into the air, landing mere feet before them, and Agnes scowled imperiously at him.

He lifted his long, clawed fingers, giggling shrilly as he dashed towards them. Agnes drew a small, bulbous brass and glass pistol from her belt and fired.

The eldritch beast spun in mid-air and collapsed unceremoniously to the forest floor. Agnes huffed in disappointment, peering at the pistol. "Papa said it was set to disintegrate." She bent over the creature, drawing several lengths of copper chains from her belt, which she used to bind him up with a discomfited expression. "He barely looks charred."

"Stun."

"Well, that is just unacceptable. How could Papa lie to me like that?"

"Besides the point."

"I think it's precisely the point, Vic! If this Spring-Heeled Jack creature is one of the voices we heard underground, a flimsy stun gun isn't going to be of much help, is it?" She prodded the creature with her boot. "I am most disappointed by this turn of events."

"Monsters?"

She stomped her foot. "Not the monsters! The monsters are brilliant. I hope there's scores more. If there are monsters, what has become of the sailors?"

"Lunch."

"Vic, that is tremendously demoralizing. Do shut up." She glanced around. "But how are we to find them?"

"Footprints."

"Vic, sometimes I astonish myself with my cleverness."

"Me."

"Who created you, anyway? Come!"

Agnes tucked the ear trumpet back into her tool belt. She did not holster her pistol, despite its unexpectedly dissatisfactory designation. She narrowed her eyes, searching for the indents the sprightly menace had made in the squishy forest floor. They were far apart, for he could leapt great distances, but they led swiftly towards an outcropping of rock near the shore. It did not appear to be an entrance to anything, but Agnes dropped to her knees, prodding the rock with the tip of her pistol.

At once, a flat, smooth stone rolled away with a grinding whir, and an opening appeared in the forest floor. Agnes yelped in delighted surprise. Vic clapped a hand over her mouth. "Discreet."

She rolled her eyes at him, but she seized the front of his ratty suit. "This must be it, Vic. This is where Spring-Heeled Jack came from, and if I am much mistaken, we will discover the fate of our lost sailors."

Vic heaved a deep, long suffering sigh, but he nodded wearily. "Caution."

"Whilst I would normally quite enjoy contradicting you, I do reckon you may have a point there."

The entrance dipped down into a long, narrow tunnel. Agnes drew a pale wand from her belt and beat it several times against a wall that felt like smooth, riveted metal. A toxic green glow illuminated the small space, revealing nothing more than hammered, patchwork metal plate walls and inky blackness ahead. The tunnel was eerily silent, and the sound of her breathing rent the vacuum, making her feel quite self-conscious, which was not a familiar or pleasant feeling.

Up ahead in the darkness, a strange, mewling sound echoed off the dull metal walls. Agnes pressed a finger to her lips, but she needn't have bothered; Vic was silent as the grave. They inched forward, and the floor dipped as the tunnel curved, plunging deeper and deeper into the sepulchral pitch.

A faint, flickering light flared at the end of the tunnel. Agnes caught her breath as excitement fluttered in her chest. She lifted the glowing wand over her face to grin at Vic. He grinned back, but not intentionally. He was, reasonably, hesitant to confront the horrors which surely lay ahead of them. Being a horror himself, he was rather unaccountably uncomfortable in the presence of others of his ilk.

Agnes hurried through the increasingly grey darkness and burst impetuously into the light.

She had no time to observe her surroundings, for her sudden appearance elicited a very strong response from the mob of beasts milling confusedly about the small, metallic antechamber into which she and Vic stepped. As one, the creatures moaned, mewled, giggled, yowled, shrieked and growled, throwing their scaly, hirsute, mottled, discoloured, colourless and horrific bodies at her in a single, terrifying movement.

Agnes did not cower or back away from the cluster of monsters. She fired her pistol in quick, rapid bursts whilst Vic flailed dangerously with his rotting limbs, fighting off the monsters. There were creatures that looked as though they had just emerged from the sea, slimy and dripping with sludgy water; men with sharp, deadly fangs and glowing eyes; wolves that wore torn clothing and stood upright like men; several more of the sprightly, clawed, cackling creatures they'd met in the forest, some with skin as red as blood or black as midnight; beasts whose skin appeared dangerously aflame; fat, wrinkled, fleshy things with tiny, beady eyes and huge, grimacing mouths; devils and demons and angels with bottomless, Stygian eyes; bogeymen that resembled neither beast nor human but something she could not identify, for they seemed to be in constant, frenetic motion and had no distinguishable features at all.

Agnes dispatched all of the horrors, and the bodies piled up in the antechamber, blocking her path. She sighed in annoyance and hoisted herself over the hideous creatures, her boot slipping on a slimy Eachy and smashing quite roughly into the nose of one of the Shug monkeys. He responded with a slight whine, but he could not extract himself from the heap to retaliate. Vic shambled after her, stumbling over the demons and several Spring-Heeled Jacks. He grunted in displeasure, but he did not complain.

Beyond the heap of stunned monster bodies, an enormous man waited, his tree trunk thick legs crouched defensively as he waited for them. His knuckles brushed the dull gunmetal grey floor, and he glared at them out of a wide, squashed face. His mouth, lined with huge, stubby teeth that looked quite suitable to chomping bones, hung open. His breath was harsh and powerful, washing over Agnes and Vic like a warm, fetid breeze.

But his eyes, those large, sparkling blue eyes were not the eyes of a monstrous giant. They were horribly, uncannily aware, the eyes of an animal trapped in an

34

enormous, hideous fleshy cage. He did not strike, did not rush her or swing his ham-sized hands at her, and Agnes stared at him speculatively for several long moments.

It struck her then. She understood. These were not monsters, or they had not been earlier that day. They had been men. She spun towards the mound of feebly flailing beasts. Yes, she could see it now. Their white uniforms were torn, shredded by the contortions of their new bodies, but she knew them all the same. Sailors. They were sailors. They were the sailors, those whom she had come to find, and she had now done.

They were in slightly worse condition than she had originally foreseen. Adjustments would have to be made. "Vic," she whispered, returning her eyes to the rapt, horrified giant. "I think these are the sailors. Something's been done to them."

"Obvious."

She opened her mouth to retort scathingly, but the giant chose that moment to take possession of his body. He roared furiously, beating his knuckles on the metal floor. They left impressions the size of a human man's feet. He bared his teeth and lowered his shoulder, rushing the small girl and her ghastly companion with deadly outstretched arms.

Agnes sighed. "I would have gone easy on you, dreg, if you'd just been politer about it." She fired her pistol, though it did little more than slow the beast's rush. She rolled her eyes and fired again right between the over-sized sailor's eyes.

The ground shook as he crashed to the ground. Agnes' pistol smoked, and she holstered it quickly, for its glass and thin brass burned her fingers. She glanced at Vic. "What do you suppose has been done to them?"

"Changed."

She huffed irritably. "That much is quite obvious, Vic. I expected something more insightful."

He lifted his shoulders, and she waved her hand dismissively, peering around them in interest. They had not, as she had expected, stepped into the heart of the underground monster-making lair. Instead, they were in a large, featureless, high-ceilinged antechamber that forked ahead, past the fallen giant, into two more tunnels like the one from which they had emerged. She sighed in dismay.

"Which way should we go?"

Vic shambled forwards, peering for a moment into each equally dark, narrow passage. He lifted his shoulders.

Agnes scoffed. "Oh, I don't know why I bother to ask you a thing. You're utterly useless."

"Took out revenant."

"That was mighty irreverent of you. You're practically kin."

Vic seemed to take offence to this. He lifted his chin. "Zombie."

"Yes, well, you are quite more sophisticated, aren't you?" She pressed a contemplative finger to her lips. Inspiration struck. She drew the ear trumpet once more from her belt, directing the disc towards the portals ahead. The first was silent and dank, but the faint sound of clanking and shrieks could be heard from the second. She perked up. "Huzzah!"

She tucked the trumpet back into her belt and drew the still slightly warm pistol. She grinned at Vic, jerking her head towards the passageway. "Shall we, then?"

He was still quite put out being compared to the bumpkinly undead revenants, but he sighed resignedly and shuffled after the green glow she spread through the dark tunnel. The sounds she'd heard through the trumpet grew louder as they drew swiftly closer. There was no light at the end of this tunnel, but a large, metal door which was dented from both sides, appearing as though something very large and very strong had battered it from inside and out. From beyond the door, she could hear a relentless, high-pitched wail and the distinct hum of machinery.

She quashed the flicker of apprehension in her belly and squared her shoulders, drawing herself up to her fullest height. She half-turned to her re-animated clockwork attendant. "Steady on, Vic. The belly of the beasts awaits."

"Rumbly."

"Yes, I suspect their bellies are rather rumbly."

"My belly."

"That's just the maggots. We'll get you sorted when we get out of here. Step lively."

The door was not barred, and she eased it open, her pistol at the ready. She needn't have concerned herself with immediate detection, for nothing bore down upon them as they crept inside the capacious chamber. It was, she realized instantly, a very well-appointed laboratory. Shelves of glowing, glutinous liquid lined the east wall, and stacks of metal, wire, glass, gears, tubes and strange tools piled up against the west. She could not see to the far wall, for in the centre of the room, dozens of gurneys occupied by the remaining sailors, apparently slumbering, obscured her view.

A man attended them, dressed in a scorched white lab coat. His hair was shock white, overlong and hanging lankly around his lined face, which was lit with keenness. His dark eyes burned behind the thick, brass goggles upon his face. His mouth twisted into a gleeful grimace. He stood over one of the gurneys, his hand lifted to the instrument above his head.

It was a very large, very elaborate apparatus, appearing much like but quite more sizeable than the average cannon, its barrel long and bulbous and constructed of thick, hazy glass and gleaming steel. Tubes protruded from its body, attached to gauges and valves. It posed upon a large, rolling tripod, and a hose connected the ominous dingus to a cylindrical chamber nearby, which was filled with a thick, roiling liquid or heavy gas substance that glowed an uncanny yellow.

Its operator gripped a smudged brass lever, yanking it towards him with an expression of delighted anticipation. The apparatus hummed briefly, then it almost shrieked as a beam of brilliant light shot from the barrel, illuminating the sleeping sailor for a brief moment in an unholy nimbus. The sailor awoke suddenly, or seemed to, for a terrible wail escaped him, and as the light faded, his body writhed and struggled frantically against the leather restraints binding him to the table.

The mad, white-haired man laughed wildly as the sailor's body rippled. Agnes cringed at the sounds of popping bones and tearing flesh. The leather bonds snapped in two as the body of the sailor contorted into something else, something horrible and hideous, a creature with skin like shining ebony with long, terrible claws and sharp, deadly teeth. It leapt from the table, leering around at the sailors on the gurneys as though they presented a suitable snack. He gnashed his teeth.

The scientist cackled. "Not yet, my pet. We still need them. They will be your brothers, but there are two intruders in our midst, of which you may make a very appetizing first meal."

He had not, as Agnes had believed, been oblivious to their intrusion.

The ebony stone skinned creature spun towards them, widening his grinding mouth in a ghastly grin. He lifted hands as long and sharp as needles and raced towards them. Agnes did not fire her pistol. Instead, she seized Vic's arm and stepped to the side, for the creature, while swift and deadly, was quite stupid. He did not anticipate their change in direction and continued on his path, battering himself against the metal door until he slid, quite insensible, to the floor.

"That explains the dents," Agnes remarked. She strode haughtily towards the abominable scientist. "What is the meaning of this, sir?"

His mouth curved down unhappily. "I see you have gotten past my children."

He eyed her curiously. "But I must say, I did not expect such a formidable intruder to be nothing more than a little girl."

She drew herself up indignantly. "I am much more than a mere little girl, as you can see."

He frowned. "Nevertheless, you should not have come."

She jabbed an accusatory finger at him. "You are stealing sailors from their ships and transforming them into monsters!"

"Very astute."

She peered around in sudden keenness. "How did you get them here? Do you have some sort of matter transporter? How do you power it? Electro-magnetic energy? Steam? Radioactive waste? Conducting the force of human misery into a viable power source? Tell me! Tell me!"

The scientist lifted an eyebrow. "You know something about matter transporters?"

She scoffed. "Oh, sure. I built one of those when I was ten, but I used the collected kinetic energy of ten thousand very disgruntled lab rats."

He peered at her in comic incredulity.

She tossed her caramel-coloured pigtails. "I can't expect others to apprehend my genius. Anyway, it only transported gerbils from one end of the room to the other, and they weren't alive when they got there. This is much more impressive."

"So you are skilled with the scientific arts?"

She smiled proudly. "My papa is the famed inventor, Dr Nimrod Crowley. He is very clever, but I am cleverer. I find ways to sneak around him all the time."

The mad man laughed and stuck out a hand swathed in yellow rubber. "I am Dr Cornelius Antonin." He looked past her at Vic, who took in the laboratory with several jerky ticks of his clockwork neck. "Did you create the revenant?"

Vic blanched. "Offensive!"

Agnes scoffed. "He isn't anything as crude as a revenant, sir, and he is quite sensitive about it. I would thank you not to insult him in future. He's a re-animated clockwork cadaver. I made him in my basement."

His grin stretched more widely, revealing large, broad teeth that were all a single size and of a very strange yellowed ivory colour. "My apologies. He is most amusing and not without some elegance, I must say. I see no reason the two of us should row, young Miss Crowley." He gestured grandly around them. "As you can see, I am quite occupied here lately. I could use a clever assistant gifted in the dubious and dark scientific arts. You, my young intruder, seem most worthy for such a position."

She stiffened indignantly. "Certainly not! I like a little sport now and again. I once turned my friend Hector into a sort of moth-man, for which I was most soundly punished and had to put him right again, which was quite disappointing, but that was an accident and he was all right after he stopped moulting. I don't do things like this. Kidnapping is wrong."

Dr Antonin sighed in deep disappointment. "That is a great shame. I would have been pleased to teach you all sorts of things about transfiguring humans into genetically enhanced super-monsters."

"Not interested."

"All right, then. Have it your way. Just remember that I did offer, and I was most sincere. It is your own fault it has come to this." He spun suddenly, jabbing a finger at Agnes and Vic as he shouted over his shoulder, "Jack!"

Dr Antonin had created an inordinate number of the sprightly masters of menace. This one had pale skin and burning red eyes. It leapt out of the shadows beyond the monster-making apparatus, its sharp, metallic claws gleaming in the brilliant overhead gaslights. Agnes rolled her eyes and raised a hand to stun this new terror in mid-air.

She turned the little brass and glass ray on the dismayed Dr Antonin. He lifted his hands. "But-my beauties! Surely someone of your keen, inquisitive mind can commiserate!"

Agnes considered this, cocking her head to the side to study him. "But what are you planning to do with all of these monsters? For what purpose did you create them?"

He looked somewhat nonplussed by this question. "To have them. Is there any greater pursuit than that of scientific knowledge and successful application?" He touched a thin finger to his lips. "Also, I thought perhaps I would turn them towards my ambition to take over the world."

She scoffed. "Naturally. You know how many of you mad world-domination crazed scientists my papa and I have thwarted?" She glared at him. "We don't like competition!"

Dr Antonin's eyes burned like mad little coals behind his goggles. He moved abruptly, shoving a gurney into the unwary little girl. It took her in the stomach, knocking the breath from her and doubling her over the inert sailor. The doctor spun and raced towards the opposite end of the laboratory, but before he made it to his destination, likely a hasty emergency escape or a self-destruct protocol initiator, Vic shambled forward with unexpected speed, seizing him by the collar and dragging him back.

He flailed, but Vic did not loosen his hold. "Cease and desist," he suggested positively.

Dr Antonin slumped in defeat. "You are remarkably strong for a revenant."

Vic shook his head in disgust, but he did not argue with the raving mad scientist. Agnes lifted her chin and faced him with a vainglorious smirk. "You have been foiled, Dr Antonin. Do not feel bad; you are not the only one to have gambled against Agnes Crowley and lost your shirt. Vic, take him."

"Bigger ship."

She sighed. "Ah, yes. I see your point. We won't be able to bring all these monsters home in that tiny canary." She pressed a finger to her lips, considering. Her caramel-coloured eyes lit up keenly. "Perhaps we could reverse the matter transporter." She turned her eyes to Antonin. "Where is it?"

He glared maliciously at her, but she ignored him, not waiting for a response. She wandered around the laboratory, fiddling idly with the equipment she found simply lying thoughtlessly around.

A flash of brilliant yellow light engulfed Vic, and for a moment, she could hear his aggravated moan. Then the sound shifted into a sort of exasperated gargle. When the light faded, Vic stood, still clutching Dr Antonin in his slimy, rotted lizard hands. His slitted, beady eyes glared at Agnes through a mottled reptilian face. He opened his mouth to speak, but a forked tongue darted past his sharp fangs instead of the scathing admonishment. He gargled unhappily.

She'd transformed him into a re-animated clockwork sea monster. She lifted her shoulders sheepishly. "Ah. My apologies, Vic. I expect that was very degrading."

Dr Antonin leaned away from the slimy Eachy cadaver, terror in his eyes. "He's venomous, you know."

"That's convenient." She cocked her head at Vic. "I don't suppose you—"

Vic gargled at her.

"No, of course. Sorry. I'll just—hm. How do I change him back?"

"You have to reverse the dial," Dr Antonin told her urgently as venom dripped from Vic's reptilian mouth, sizzling on the metal floor, so near the man's boot, he yelped in fear.

"Not so enamoured of your beauties now, are you?" Agnes said smugly.

"He is not a beauty! He is a revenant bog creature, and he is sloughing all over me!"

Agnes sniggered at Vic's indignation and examined the monster ray. "Ah. I see now." The large dial of which the doctor spoke pointed quite clearly towards Glorious Monstrosity. She spun it back to Dismally Dull Human, though Vic was none of those things, and jerked the lever down. The blinding light enveloped Vic once more, and when it faded, he stood, quite himself, once more.

Dr Antonin sighed in relief, but Vic looked down at his ratty figure in slight disappointment. Being venomous had been, momentarily, rather fraught with possibility. He had little time to consider his continuing misfortune; there were more pressing matters at hand.

"Which one of these mad dinguses is the matter transporter?" Agnes demanded, fiddling with the volatile cylinders of toxic liquids, the ill-conceived engines, the particle accelerators and the directed energy rays she found scattered haphazardly around the laboratory. She pressed a button on a hopeful looking wave cannon, and a beam of poisonous green light shot from its barrel, disintegrating a rack of test tubes filled with murky grey sludge.

"Stop that! Stop mucking with things!" Dr Antonin cried desperately. "You're going to ruin everything!"

Agnes shot him an arch look. "You'd best help, then, I reckon. Where is the matter transporter?"

He pressed his lips together with a stubborn gleam in his dark eyes.

"Right, then. I'll just keep mucking about, then, eh?" She stopped dead in her tracks, her eyes widening agog. "Ooh. What's this?"

She stepped towards a large, cylindrical glass chamber that spanned from floor to ceiling, its diameter at least as wide as her bedroom closet laboratory at home in the Crowley Tower of Astonishing Innovations and Brilliant Discoveries, so named by her pompous, infamously mad papa. The chamber was not the most astonishing feature, for it was just one of two constructed side-by-side along the far wall of Antonin's laboratory. Rather, it was the large chamber of moving, multi-coloured energy housed in between the two empty chambers that tickled her fancy.

"Wicked!" She pressed her nose to the glass, watching the liquidised energy swirl and swish in the thick glass chamber.

"Stay away from there!"

She ignored the raving doctor and directed her attention to the collection of dials and gauges protruding from the base of the chamber. They looked much like those on the Brass Canary, and she suspected they worked in much the same way. She examined the display of strange numbers on a small scrap of ticker tape. "What are these?"

"Get away from there! You don't know what you're doing! You'll ruin everything!"

Vic dragged him towards the chambers, eyeing the read out curiously. "Coordinates."

"Vic, you re-animated genius! They are coordinates." She frowned. Admiring the ingenuity of the apparatus, she located the dials, spinning them at random to see the ticker tape spit out the exact coordinates she had entered.

"It's very delicate!"

"This won't help us much," Agnes remarked unhappily. "I don't know anything about latitude and longitude."

Vic's milky eyes rolled back into his head. He thrust a thick pile of parchment he'd picked up from a side table into her hands.

She peered down at the stack in confusion until she made sense of the cryptic symbols and sweeping criss-crossing lines. "A map! Vic! Why didn't I think of this?"

He scoffed, but he did not trouble himself to retort.

After several painstaking moments in which Dr Antonin watched her in smug silence, she spun the dials, grinning eagerly up at the energy chamber. It glowed violently, swirling with a frenetic vim that seemed almost lifelike. "Brilliant! Let's see if we got the coordinates right. We can zap the doctor and bring him back." She screwed her face up thoughtfully. "I only hope it doesn't turn out like the gerbils. I was quite confident about them, too."

Vic tugged on his arm, and Dr Antonin dragged his heels. "Stop! I—" He hung his head in a last, forlorn gesture of defeat. "I will show you."

Agnes beamed at him. "Okay. Thanks!"

He submitted to Vic, who tugged on his arm. He spun the dials with intense concentration, pressing buttons and eyeing the gauges carefully. He sighed in relief when he'd righted the shambles the little girl had wrought upon his beloved device.

"Set it to send us back to Kelpie Wharf," Agnes commanded imperiously.

He turned a scowl upon her. "I will not do that. I will send you all out to sea."

Her smile did not falter; if anything, it was more radiant than ever. "All right. You go first. Vic?"

Vic propelled him towards one of the empty chambers. Antonin held up his

42

hands, squealing in terror. "All right! All right! I will show you how to set it correctly."

"Thanks" She watched as he consulted the map coordinates and spun the dials. Vic eyed his handiwork speculatively, then nodded to Agnes. "Great! Now, you and Vic go first. He'll lash you to the railing or something equally clever, and then I'll bring him back."

Vic did not like the sound of this. "Spliced."

She rolled her eyes in exasperation. "You're not going to get spliced! Just don't move. I'll give you a few moments to bind him up really good, and then I'll zap you right back here. If you aren't ready, just don't step back into the beam, and I'll take a stray dog or some village riff-raff instead."

Vic heaved a deep, long-suffering sigh, but he stepped into the empty chamber, dragging the pleading, wide-eyed mad man along with him. "Justice."

"That's right, Dr Antonin, Vic will explain everything to my father when we get back, and you will be sorry. Ready Vic?"

"Keen."

"Ace." She slammed the glass chamber door shut with a snap and gleefully cranked the dial on the operator panel. "Right, then, old chap, see you in a mo'"

The energy churned and battered the walls of its chamber, and a loud, almost deafening whine filled the air, rattling the laboratory walls. In a flash of light, Vic and his unfortunate captive were gone. Agnes spun back around to admire the doctor's impressive accomplishments. Left alone to Dr Antonin's devices, she could not resist another go with the directed energy cannon. Or the human transmuter or the cyclotron, or the really brilliant hand-held guns that performed a variety of very hilarious functions, such as slightly altering the length of the sailors' noses or their hair or changing the colour of their skin or giving them really hideous buck teeth or...

She stopped dead, glancing sheepishly at the small pocket watch tucked into a breast pocket of her lab coat. She'd quite forgotten to zap Vic back in all the excitement. She hurried to the matter transporter and reversed the direction. Light flashed once again, and a very irritated-looking Vic glared out at her through the thick, shining glass.

"Sorry, sorry!" She strode forward to throw open the door. "I got a bit... carried away."

"Shiny?"

"Oh, so many shiny things! Look! This little gun here turns his arms into--" She subsided at the stern look on her companion's face. "All right, all right. I

43

hope you left the doctor somewhere safe."

"Constable."

"Spot on, Vic. Spot on. Right. Now." She turned towards the laboratory playground, suddenly seized with the urge to throw herself into its shiny delights, but she steeled her resolve. "We've got to get these sailors home. We'll have to get them into the matter transporter."

"Ship?"

"Don't be ridiculous. This is much more entertaining."

"Heavy."

"Stop complaining. There's only about fifty of them."

"Seventy."

"Well, who's counting, anyway? Right then. Step lively."

It took more time than she'd anticipated to drag all the stunned monsters from the heap in the antechamber to the transporter's chamber, and they panted with the effort when they'd done. The monsters, transmuted as they were to ghastly inhuman proportions and contortions, did not quite fit. The glass door did not close behind them.

Agnes stomped her foot in irritation. "We'll have to send them a few at a time," she complained, dragging the mob back out of the chamber again. They sent them back to Port Enshus a half-dozen or so at a time, space permitting.

"Havoc," Vic moaned apathetically.

"Belt up! I'm not wreaking havoc. They're all knocked out. It's fine. They're the villagers' loved ones. It's a perfectly reasonable solution to the problem."

Vic shrugged as they hefted the last of the monsters, several semi-identical Spring-Heeled Jacks, and watched them disappear in a flash of light. "Canary?"

"No!" Agnes glared at him. "You've already gotten to ride it. It's my turn. I'll set the dial on a delay. I've become quite good at this matter transporting thing in the last hour or so. Come on, then." She seized his arm and dragged him inside the chamber with her, closing the door behind them. She waited eagerly, and then the light flashed, and she felt a strange floating sensation, as though every particle in her body had come completely apart, leaving only her twisted mind intact. Before she even had a moment to revel in the intriguing sensation, her parts came back together and she was righted again, blinking around at foggy Kelpie Wharf.

The scene into which they transported was quite ghastly, which she might have anticipated, had she spent more time thinking through her choices, rather than choosing the more amusing path.

The monsters, enervated from their temporary torpor, rampaged through the town, shrieking, howling, yowling, gurgling, biting, slashing and terrorising the poor, unsuspecting fishy villagers, who battled their loved ones with harpoons, six-shooters, axes and bits of broken buildings they'd picked up in the melee.

"Havoc," Vic said in a very smug way.

Agnes ignored him. She threw herself into the mayhem, calling out to the murderous villagers. "Don't kill them! Don't kill them! They are your friends and loved ones! It isn't their fault a mad scientists transmuted them into legendary monsters in his misguided ambition to take over the world! It's all of a piece! This isn't the way civilised people behave, you mad, savage imbeciles!"

It was as though her supplications fell on deaf ears. She could not imagine why. The villagers kept right on fighting, and the monsters kept right on rampaging.

"Stop! Stop!" She found Luther in the madness, his mouth twisted in a primal snarl as he leapt upon a giggling goblin, raising a spear over his head. "Luther, you must get a hold of yourself!"

They were all behaving very childishly and very unreasonably. No one seemed interested in her very sensible explanation. She sighed deeply. Vic lifted his shoulders smugly. She glared at him.

"Well, reasoning with them is right out." She fumbled for her belt and found the small, shining metal sphere she'd tucked away for just such an occasion but was most disappointed to be parted with; she had been hoping to save it for a special occasion, such as one of her papa's more boring parties where the most prominent scientists of the day were standing around eating cheese, drinking port and droning on as they tried to one-up each other for the most impressive innovation of the season.

She raced into the centre of town, where the expo had been disrupted by the arrival of three score or more hideous, blood-thirsty monsters. The booths and displays had been upturned and lay trampled beneath dozens of large, hairy behemoth feet. She yanked her goggles down over her eyes and slapped her trusty mufflers over her ears. Then she tossed the sphere down onto the ground with all her might, right in the very heart of the scrimmage.

Vic clapped his hands over his ears as a boom so loud it was nearly inaudible rippled through the shanty town in waves of concussing sound. The monsters and maddened villagers alike dropped instantly where they stood in a confusion of human and mutated limbs. Agnes sighed in the sudden quiet that engulfed them. Then she giggled. The concussion grenade was quite fun, really. She ought to nick more from her papa's store of interesting inventions or at least lay hands upon his designs. She was certain she could improve the range of the clever little device with a bit of tinkering and reckless experimentation that could, if luck was with her, potentially result in permanent damage to the dreadful neighbours' youngest, ill-mannered son...

Vic's mouth turned down in dread. "Crowley."

Agnes sighed. "I know, I know. He'll be very cross when he comes to, and we'll have to explain everything. Anyway, no sense in worrying about it now. We have to sort out how to swap those sailors back--"

"No. Crowley." Vic lifted a hand to point over her shoulder.

With a sense of impending doom, Agnes turned slowly on her heel. Dr Crowley, his hands propped on his hips, glowered imperiously down at her in the midst of the devastation. "Agnes..." He did not bark or snap or shout, but his low, dangerous tone was quite indicative of the intensity of his disapproval. His voice was soft when he spoke. "What did I tell you about dropping concussion bombs in small villages?"

She didn't meet his eyes. She scuffed her toe on the ground. "I don't know. I don't remember you telling me anything about that--"

"Agnes! We had this discussion not two months ago. Don't pretend you don't remember it. I remember quite clearly that I demanded you return all the concussion bombs you stole from me the last time. Do you expect me to believe you simply forgot about this one?"

"No, I--" Her shoulders slumping in defeat. "Sorry, Papa."

"You will be sorry when I get through with you."

She lifted her eyes to scowl at him. "How did you escape it, anyway?"

"Never leave home without your protective film and preventative accoutrements." He rolled his eyes and yanked a flesh coloured plug from inside his ear. He lifted a sardonic eyebrow. "After the last time, I thought it best to be prepared. I expected something like this. You are in big trouble, young lady."

"But I can explain! I had no choice, Papa! I was helping stop the villagers from killing their loved ones who've been transmuted into monsters by a mad, unscrupulous scientist! I was helping!"

"Helping," he repeated, looking around at the men and beasts scattered at their feet. "Transmuted into monsters, you say?" He bent to examine an Eachy. "I see." He straightened to look at her. "Would you care to explain how you came across these mutant monsters and how exactly they ended up rampaging through town?"

"Oh, yes!" She launched into an explanation of wandering into the tavern, in which she'd learned of the Kelpie Wharf, and of the mysterious ghost ships arriving without their crews. Dr Crowley's expression did not change, but his eyes flickered as she described their discovery of Dr Antonin's ostensibly serene island, their scuffle with Spring-Heeled Jack in the forest, then the mob they'd encountered in the antechamber of Antonin's underground monster-making lair. He did not appear to be impressed, even as she detailed her impressive victory over the legendary terrors of Europe and beyond and her defeat of their barmy, misguided Maker.

He pursed his lips. "Mm," he murmured disdainfully. "Another world-domination scheme, then?"

"I think he was mostly just lonely. Anyway, he has some very brilliant devices. I think we could use his transfiguration dingus to change the monsters back into sailors."

"Sailors?"

"Oh, yes, didn't I mention? All these monsters, they're the missing sailors from the Aqueous Spectre and the Wraith Alloy." She rolled her eyes with equal disdain. "Or didn't you sort that out on your own?"

"Right. And you didn't think to come find me before you went dashing off on some mad chase to an abandoned island after the missing sailors?"

She lifted her chin. "I didn't need your help. I managed quite well. I did, after all, defeat a mob."

He sighed. "I'll just have a closer look at them."

Agnes hovered impatiently over her papa as he examined a revenant nearby. He surged to his feet, nodding decisively. "I think we'd best get them back to the lab."

"What? After all the trouble I went through to get them here?"

"Helped," Vic added, but they ignored him.

"Can't we just bring the transmuter here?"

"That would be ill-advised. We can't be certain of its functionality outside a laboratory environment. You oughtn't to have brought them here." He lifted an eyebrow. "How did you get them all here, anyway?"

She beamed smugly. "A matter transporter."

He looked quite keen on this idea. "Really? It worked?"

"Oh, aye. It was very exciting. I got to ride on it. We could use it again, I suppose."

He peered around at the heaps of monsters and their kin. "Right. We'll have to get them all back to the point of entry. Do you have the remote for the device?"

Her shoulders slumped. "No. If there was one, Dr Antonin did not bother to share."

"Hardly unexpected. We'll have to return to the island, then, to trigger the device from its source."

She nodded eagerly, but her expression transformed into one of dismay as he crossed his arms over his chest and glowered pointedly at her. "What?"

"I suggest you begin gathering up these beasts if we intend to put them right before your concussion wears off."

"What? But—by myself?"

"Yes."

She stomped her foot. "But it's so hard! They're so heavy!"

"You ought to have thought of that before you dragged them all here. You will have plenty of time to consider the consequence of your rash and foolish lack of judgment. I expected better of the clever fruit of my loins. Now drag these bodies into a pile on the wharf."

She grunted in frustration, seizing the arms of an Eachy. She glared up at her papa. "You could help, you know."

"Oh, yes. I could. I even have a pocket transporter that could zap them all quite quickly to the wharf, but I think this is the best punishment for your behaviour."

"I'm not the one who made the monsters! I was trying to help!" She pouted. "I'm only twelve. I don't always make the right choices. Aren't parents supposed to help their children learn from their mistakes?"

"Oh, indeed they are, and that is exactly what I am doing. Get to it. No more complaints."

He watched, his hands propped on his hips, as his daughter and her re-animated clockwork companion dragged the bodies back to the pier, huffing and puffing with their exertion. It was slow, tiring work, but it was done eventually, and Dr Crowley nodded in satisfaction.

"Now what?" Agnes asked breathlessly.

"Where is this island of yours, then?"

"Not far. About a kilometre out to sea."

"Excellent! I'll drive." He lifted a finger to point at the walking cadaver. "You wait here, Vic, and feed the monsters into the transporter."

Vic knew better than to make a snide remark to the revered doctor, for his continued existence relied upon the man's indulgence. He nodded stiffly.

Agnes followed her father to his shiny gold hot air balloon and watched as he prepared the vessel for the short flight, igniting the ballonet and inflating the envelop with an ease that came from much practise. He hoisted her into the gondola, and the airship lifted smoothly off the ground.

Agnes glared sourly down at the gentle waves as they floated swiftly across the water towards Antonin's island. Dr Crowley alighted beside the Brass Canary. "Ah," he said in a deceptively light voice. "I see you commandeered a ship for your journey. I don't remember this one being part of our fleet."

She scowled. "I did not commandeer it. It was offered to me."

They continued to bicker as she led him unerringly towards the outcropping of rock that concealed the entrance to the underground lair. Her father continued to scold her for her lack of foresight as they descended into the sepulchral dankness of the tunnels. A large, hairy beast lay prone in the tunnel, blocking the light of the antechamber.

Dr Crowley lifted a questioning eyebrow at his daughter.

She scuffed her toe sheepishly. "Ah. We must have forgotten this one," she admitted in a small voice.

He rolled his eyes, seizing the Shug monkey's wrist and dragging him along as they continued towards the laboratory. "Bloody hell, Agnes. Everywhere you go, I end up having to clean up after you."

She stomped her foot. "I told you! I am not the one who made the monsters! I just protected myself and tried to save the village."

"Bang up job, darling."

When they reached Antonin's laboratory, her father forgot to be cross with her. His gleaming eyes took in the surroundings and innovations with keen fascination. Agnes thought perhaps the venerable old genius was rather impressed. He likely would have enjoyed the mad doctor's company, had Vic not prematurely thrust him into the arms of the local constabulary. She resolved to tell him off for it later.

"This is the matter transporter?" Unlike Agnes, he had recognised the apparatus instantly, though he had, admittedly, lost out on the entertaining exploration of the lab's additional offerings. He stared at the device for several long moments. His hands flew over the operator panel. "Ah, yes. I see how it works."

He did not ask her advice on its proper operation, though she thought she was quite more suited to the current task, considering her familiarity with the machine. Nevertheless, she did not argue as her father reversed the directional dial and pressed the button. Instantly, light flooded the empty chamber and faded to reveal a pile of monsters. "Very good. Very good indeed," he muttered to himself. "Agnes!"

She did not require direction. She knew precisely what he expected of her. She dragged the bodies out of the chamber and piled them unceremoniously on the floor. Somewhere, she sensed Vic's commiseration as he prepared the next delivery of transmuted sailors, which her father zapped presently back to the laboratory. When they'd all returned, her father turned his attention to the transmutation device. Or rather, turned his attention to locating it.

Agnes opened her mouth and lifted her hand to direct her father towards the proper machine, but he lifted a hand to forestall her. He was quite keen to explore the laboratory and its accoutrements. He located the monster-maker quite quickly, and his eyes gleamed in admiration as he stroked its bulbous barrel and its polished brass bits.

Presently, Agnes grew bored with the proceedings. She stepped stealthily to the side, picking up one of the hand-held wave guns she hadn't gotten an opportunity to examine. She aimed it at the Shug monkey and fired. He grunted in his sleep as his ears, already quite long and pointed, grew to twice their length, terminating in sharp, deadly tips.

Dr Crowley spun on her in irritation. "Agnes! Put that down now."

She sighed, dropped the gun at her side. It clattered against the hammered metal floor. "Fine."

"I am ready. Bring me the first monster."

"The device is on wheels, you know."

"That is beside the point. Step lively."

She huffed as she dragged the Shug monkey to the gurney. Her father did not assist her in hoisted it up onto the flat, thin mattress. When the creature was strapped down, her papa directed the beam directly over him and yanked gleefully down on the lever. The beam of light flashed over the body, and Crowley watched curiously as it faded.

The sailor, quite roguish-looking in his torn clothes but otherwise quite ordinary in appearance, blinked up at them in hazy confusion. He looked around, then down at this bound wrists. He rolled his eyes between them.

"What's going on? Am I in hospital? Did something happen to the ship?"

"No. You were brought here by a matter transporter and turned into a monster by a mad scientist," Agnes explained, bored already.

The sailor seemed not to know what to say. He eyed Dr Crowley uneasily.

Agnes rolled her eyes. "Not that mad scientist. A different one. This one just changed you back."

"Right." He didn't seem to believe them, for apparently he did not retain the memories of his Shug monkey self. All the better for him, likely. "Can I go?"

"How do you feel?" Crowley asked, bending over him in interest.

"I feel fine. Fit. Seaworthy. Can I go?"

"You'll have to queue up by the matter transporter. We can't take you all in our ships," Agnes explained, waving her hand in the general direction of the chambers, where the pile of monsters still lay prone. "You're the first."

He stared at them in confusion as they unbuckled the restraints. "I don't really understand."

"You will in a moment," Crowley promised.

"If you don't mind terribly, you could help," Agnes told him sourly, gesturing towards the pile. "This will be much easier with two."

"Agnes," Crowley warned.

"What? It counts as doing it on my own if I dupe the help into it myself," she protested.

He rolled his eyes. "Fine. Get on with it, then."

The sailor assisted her to drag the next monster to the gurney and watched in horrified fascination as the man underwent the same treatment. Things progressed more rapidly as the sailors emerged from their monster selves and presented their crewmen for treatment. Agnes did not mind; she faded into the background, trying not to be noticed by her father as she took up her ministrations upon Antonin's unexplored store of exciting innovations.

The ostensible serenity of the moment did not last, for nothing truly good lasts forever.

The monsters were stirring, and only half had been put right again.

Dr Crowley did not bother with the fight. He watched, unmoved, as his daughter and the newly restored sailors battled their kin. Agnes fended off a dozen revenants, werewolves, vampires, demons and reptilian beats with her stun gun. The sailors punched and kicked and struck out with whatever they could lay their hands upon. Crowley sighed in irritation; there was little time for this, and the monsters couldn't very well be put back to rights when they were stampeding about, smashing up the equipment he needed.

At length, he heaved a long-suffering sighed and stepped forwards. "Everyone human, duck!"

He did not give them the opportunity to obey. Instead he drew the tiny, flat metallic disc he kept in his tool belt for just such occasions, depressing the single button in the centre of the device and releasing a concussion wave so powerful, the walls around them shook violently, threatening to come unhinged.

"There now. I prefer to work in peace, not in all that bedlam," he said in satisfaction, peering around as the sailors stared, wide-eyed at the fallen monsters around them. Some were the bit worse for wear, but they hurried to complete the task they'd begun, dragging their brethren to the doctor for transmutation.

Agnes marched over to him and glared. "What is that? Where did you get it?"

He smirked. "I invented it, of course, darling. Those grenades you nicked were merely prototypes. A single use concussion bomb is of little use to anyone. These can be used more than once, provided they are afforded the opportunity to recharge after each use."

She hurried forward with wide eyes, but he slapped her hand away and held the device over his head. "And don't think I haven't taken precautions against your thievery. We aren't finished here. As you were."

Soon the sailors outnumbered the monsters, and they made quick work of turning those remaining to rights. When they had done, Dr Crowley allowed Agnes to return them home in the matter transporter in droves of a half-dozen or more. The last sailor waved at them through the glass with an expression that could not be considered grateful. No, in fact, it appeared as though he had never been happier to see the last of someone.

"Well," Crowley said. "I think our work here is done. Let us be off. There is after all, an exposition going on, and I am much sought after."

Agnes looked around the lab in dismay. "Can't we just take a few of these--"

"No. You will have none of them. Consider it merited punishment."

"I helped!"

"Nevertheless, you are aware that you are not permitted to meddle with mad scientists without supervision. How many times do we have to have this conversation, Agnes?"

She sighed in disappointment, but she did not argue. "Sorry, Papa."

"See that it does not happen again."

They did not speak any further as they traversed the dark tunnels beneath the monster island, each perhaps contemplating the treasures they'd left behind in the lab or the unfair punishments they'd received for merely attempting to solve a very interesting mystery—and doing a bang up job of it, by the way. She should have at least gotten to keep the nose gun. It would have been quite the hit at their next cocktail party.

As he climbed into his gondola and Agnes took her place at the helm of the Brass Canary, her father called out to her. "Oh, and Agnes, one more thing."

She glanced sharply at him, already dreading his next words.

"You're grounded." With that, he lifted up into the air, and the gold balloon drifted off towards Port Enshus.

She groaned and steered the jolly boat after him, grumbling to herself all the way. Vic awaited her on Kelpie Wharf, looking as weary as it was possible for a cadaver to appear without actually being dead. "Punished?"

She glared at him angrily, then she slumped and heaved a deep sigh. "Grounded."

"Deserved."

"You won't be saying that when I can't get you that lady cadaver I promised."

He looked stricken. "So lonely."

"Tell me about it." They trudged forlornly along the foggy, weathered wharf, side by side in their misery. After a moment, she peered at him. "Well, that explains all the ghosts, I reckon."

Vic was silent a moment. "Maybe." His moan conveyed doubt.

But just then, something flickered in the fog ahead. A very beautiful woman, her long hair blowing out behind her, floated towards them out of the mist. She opened her mouth, and the sweetest, saddest lament poured from somewhere deep inside her. She lifted a hand to them, as though in supplication, and a spectral tear streaked down her cheek. Agnes could see the faintest impression of the village through her translucent, shimmering body.

Agnes nudged Vic gleefully. "Vic!" She did not speak loudly, for she did not wish to startle the vision before them. "Look! It's her! Luther was telling the truth. Kelpie Wharf really is haunted."

"Siren," Vic muttered, and his mouth turned down in a gloomy frown.

"Come on! We could bust that ghost easy!"

He shook his head firmly. "Grounded."

"Ah, Vic! At least let me find out if she's all gassy."

"Grounded."

She stomped her foot, glowered between Vic and the crooning ghost, who did not approach closer but seemed to be beckoning them to step nearer to her. Agnes ignored her and strode right past, scowling. "Fine."

The ghostly woman spun in mid-air to watch them go with a sulky expression.

"See if I ever do a good deed again," Agnes complained. "I saved all those sailors from becoming monster slaves to a raving lunatic, and all I got was punishment. That lunatic did give me an idea, though. Vic, how would you feel about a whole army of re-animated clockwork cadavers?"

Vic sighed wearily. "Created a monster."

THE END

www.ingramcontent.com/pod-product-compliance
Lightning Source LLC
Chambersburg PA
CBHW020604130626
46552CB00007B/3037